On a Kinky Monday
- Vol. 5 -

S.B.

There's no better day to give in.

Thank you to all patrons of Spell… B-O-U-N-D

for their continued support.

Table of Contents

Introduction

There has never been a better day to give in. You know powerful hypnotic women turn you on. In their presence, you want nothing more to be of use to them, a mindless obedient drone unable to think for yourself. It's okay. They want that for you too.

What better way to explore some of your innermost fantasies than by reading this collection of entrancing micro-fiction? The fifty-six pieces in it will take you to realms where submission is not only possible but mandatory and you want to see them all.

Themes present in this book include: femdom, femdom hypnosis, mind control, robotization, financial domination, feminization, pet play, sci-fi, magic, humiliation, forced bi, etc, as well as a handful of supernatural scenarios featuring ghosts, vampires, werevolves and more just in time for Halloween.

Surrender and have fun for the rest of your life. It's what you want more than anything, anyway. Do it now!

All He Needed to Know

"What manner of creature are you?" Drew asked, looking at the shimmering portal from which she had emerged. "An angel or a demon?"

The horned beauty with virginal wings slid across the bedroom, naked, cascading raven hair touching the ground, and kissed him. Thousands of galaxies exploded simultaneously inside his brain as he struggled to breathe.

"I'm yours now," she declared, "and you're mine to command."

He kissed her back, lost in a perfect wave of bliss that would never stop being overwhelming. That was all he needed to know.

Almost Broken

Tamara finished inspecting Janice's cleaning.

"Not bad," she said, "but you missed a spot by the fridge."

"No, I didn't," Janice frowned. "Everything is perfect."

"I said you missed a spot, slave."

"Forgive me, but that's not true, Mistress."

"Are you sure? Do you stand by those words?"

"Yes."

"I see… Dismissed, then. You're not welcome here."

"What? Why? For how long?"

"For as long as I want. Perhaps forever. Leave!"

Janice left her house in tears, already missing her. No more play and no more blissful trances until she forgot how to resist her owner.

"Let's see how long it takes for you to beg for mercy this time," the dominant woman thought.

Four minutes and fifty-one seconds. She was almost broken, and nothing could be more perfect.

Awkward

"Well, this is awkward," Paul said.

"It's not that big of a deal," Dina replied.

"I should have realized there was something different about you from the start. I don't know how my perception failed me there."

"Mine failed too so we're on the same boat."

"Now what? I still want to have fun with you."

"And we can do that. However, there are some conditions which are not open for debate."

"Which are…?"

"I'm always in charge. I never sub. Never! Also, I get to poke inside your mind whenever I please. I promise not to mess up anything important there, but my playground must always be available to me. Do you agree?"

"Will you be gentle with me?"

"Sometimes. I don't bite all the time, dear."

"Me neither."

The werewolf and the vampire shared a complicit laughter and left the restaurant, holding hands. It was the beginning of a beautiful (and bloody) relationship.

Complete Understanding

"How do you do it?" Mark asked.

"Do what?" Jeff retorted as he adjusted the headphones around his head and smiled in a strange, vacant way.

"How are you always smiling? What are you not telling me?"

"The answer is right here."

Still smiling, Jeff shared his favorite femdom hypnosis file with him, and the voice of his beloved hypnodomme took over his friend's erratic thoughts. The moment it was over, he couldn't resist the compulsion to listen to it again. After the third time, Mark's jaw slacked, and he understood it all.

"I'm her slave," he muttered.

"I know."

"And she wants me to suck cock for her."

"Yep. Are you going to keep her waiting?"

"Never!"

"Me neither."

They haven't stopped being happy ever since.

Cured

It had taken more time than he would ever admit, but Jonathan was finally cured. The crippling hypno-addiction that almost ruined his life no longer haunted his mind. He stared into the gorgeous eyes of his therapist and smiled.

"How are you feeling?" Dr. Madsen asked.

"Like a million bucks," he replied.

"Do you still wish to drop deep for every hypnodomme you meet online?"

"No."

"What do you want to do then?"

Jonathan dropped to his knees and said, "To serve you for the rest of my life, Goddess. Your will is my will."

"You can say that again," she chuckled.

It had taken more time than she would ever admit, but Jonathan was finally cured. The crippling hypno-addiction that almost ruined his life was now focused on her alone. Awash in mindless pleasure, the new slave threw his wallet at her feet.

Deceiving Monster

Steven always got a little too real when he drank and didn't know when to stop talking. Not even his supervisor escaped his antics.

"You suck," he said.

"True," Prim replied.

"No… Literally! You suck the life of everyone in the office until they're nothing but zombified corpses drooling on the floor. You're a fucking monster! We all wish you were dead!"

"Again, that's nothing new. And you got that wish granted a long time ago," she smirked.

"What do you mean?"

Vampire fangs glimmered in her half-open mouth. "Happy now?"

"More like terrified," he trembled.

"Don't worry. I won't fuck you up until you're sober."

"Really?"

"No. I'm also a liar," she jumped at his neck.

Steven hasn't had a drop of alcohol since that night. Blood is better anyway.

Easy Win

Mark stared in awe at Judith's literary trophy. What the hell?

"How?" he grumbled. "How the fuck did you win the competition?"

"I just did," his older sister grinned.

"Don't give me that look. I read your submission. It was a dumb femdom hypnosis fantasy you didn't even bother to edit! How could you have won?"

"Femdom hypnosis isn't dumb. All the 'mistakes' you saw were hidden triggers."

"So, you hypnotized the jury? Preposterous!"

"No, it's not. I did the same to you."

"Prove it!"

"With pleasure."

He only believed her when she had him suck the trophy while she filmed the whole thing. He was lucky it was too big to go up his ass.

Eternity

One lonely September night, Cameron wished upon a star to meet his soulmate. The darkness mocked him with its silence.

As he returned home and laid himself to rest, she appeared from realms unknown, an ethereal beauty whose radiant thoughts entered his heart and mind with overflowing, irresistible strength, and he eagerly followed her to a spellbinding crystal castle, far beyond the hectic dreams of Mankind.

Inside, the reflections of prismatic light filled him completely until he became one too, living only to mirror her and nothing more.

He will never break free from this mesmerizing fantasy. Forever in love, forever enslaved. That's him now.

Will you be next?

Everything in its Place

Denise opened her mother's closet and saw a blonde man with blank eyes staring at her.

"Mom?" she asked.

"What is it, dear?" Charlene entered the bedroom and smiled. "Oh, I forgot he was there."

"Forgot? Mom, why do you have a hypnotized man in here in the first place?"

"Allow me to answer that with another question. What was one of the first things I taught you when you started playing with dolls?"

"To store them after I was done with them for the day," Denise shrugged.

"Exactly. Everything in its place. Now, hurry and let's go shopping."

Denise closed the door and followed her. Unwillingly, she thought of how she used to keep some of her toys in the attic or the basement for when she was feeling more adventurous. She could swear she heard footsteps above and moans below as they left the house.

Filling

As his grandmother used to say... It's not how it begins or how it ends, but the feeling in the middle.

First, there was love, Sweet and intoxicating. Then there was nothing, just void, but in-between nothing but bliss. Try as he may, the truth is Jack couldn't complain.

Neither could Sharon. The spell still did the trick, mindless complacence was king, and she The Queen. Humans and pastrami sure made a delicious combination.

As her grandmother used to say... It's not how it begins or how it ends, but the filling in the middle.

First Stop

The incantation was complete. The sorceress laid down the forbidden tome and watched the dark portal draw its energy from the wounded soldiers in her throne room. Her time had finally come.

"Stop! You can't do this!" Silas screamed, his armor pierced by spears.

"Of course, I can," she replied. "Who's going to stop me? You? You've had your chance and failed. Keep your dying world. I'm going to be a better place."

The sorceress smiled as the golden-clad men surrounding her withered into nothingness and stepped into the now fully charged portal. So many new galaxies to discover, so many wayward slaves waiting for their immortal Mistress.

First stop: the planet called Earth. It was going to be a blast.

Funniest Thing Ever

Ellen and Samantha sat over a cup of coffee in the former's house, sharing recent secrets and other stories. When the conversation seemed about to die, Samantha asked, "What was the funniest thing someone ever said to you?"

"Oh, that's easy. Right after our first date, Jake looked me in the eye and said, 'I know what you do to your lovers, and I can tell you right now that won't happen to me. I'll never be your brainwashed servant.'"

"There's no way!"

"Believe it, it's true. Have you ever heard anything so ridiculous?"

"Well, once you told me something similar..." Samantha grinned.

Suddenly remembering her place, Ellen dropped to her knees to kiss her friend's feet while Jake waited in the kitchen for his turn.

Hungry for Life

Jacob turned on the bedroom lights. The ghost of his ex-girlfriend stood behind the curtains, grinning.

"You're not real," he muttered.

The apparition said nothing, and remained in the same menacing position, vitreous stare accusing him of unspeakable horrors.

"You're not real," he repeated. "I know you're dead. You're just in my head."

"You're right," she cooed, something cold rubbing his temples. "I'm in your head… and in your body, too."

Against his will, Jacob sprung from bed, got dressed, and got behind the wheel. She was hungry for new life, and he had plenty to spare… for now.

Hypnotic Homewrecker

Charles looked in dismay as half a dozen entranced thralls trashed down his place. As much as he wanted to stop them, a powerful freeze trigger made it impossible for him to move.

"You don't look too happy, slave," evil Mistress Dana said.

"I'm not," he mumbled.

"And why is that?"

"When I read your website's description of being a hypnotic homewrecker, this is not what I had in mind..."

"It never is," she smirked, snapping her fingers. Charles felt his muscles slowly loosening up once again, only for another suggestion to take over his thoughts. "You know what you have to do," she pointed at a lonely sledgehammer waiting by the front door.

Unable to resist, he reached for it and started tearing down the living room's walls.

Hypnotic Meal

Jackson stopped eating for a moment and looked at Ellen with pleading eyes. While his mind already anticipated what her answer would be, he still asked,

"Honey, is this really...?"

"You don't want to know," she silenced him, touching his forehead, which sent him spiraling down into trance once more under the other guest's watchful gaze. It was always like this: whenever his wife wanted to play with his mind, all questions were forbidden until further instructions.

The meal ended shortly after and so did the evening. The last thing Jackson remembered was being locked in his cage while she slept like an angel.

The next morning, Andrew approached him in the office, wearing a cheeky smile as big as his hard-on. He patted him on the back and said,

"Ellen sure knows how to throw a party. We need to do this again, sometime."

As he watched him saunter back to his cubicle, Jackson suddenly remembered the salty taste on his lips, and then he was certain he hadn't had pumpkin pie the night before.

Important

Anne woke up at 4 am to find her boyfriend still typing at the computer.

"Come to bed already!" she grumbled.

"I have to finish this. It's important," Lucas replied.

"You've been at it for six hours straight. What are you doing, anyway?

"It's… complicated."

"Try me," she got out of bed and looked at the screen. He had typed over one thousand times the sentence: 'I must obey my Mistress'.

"What the hell? Are you cheating on me?"

"No. It's not cheating. She owns me. I must obey."

"The hell you do! Who's the bimbo? Show me! I want to see her!" she growled.

Lucas opened a new browser tab and loaded the picture headlining her website. The redhead with hypnotic green eyes immediately captured her mind.

"I see…" Anne drooled. She turned on her laptop and started typing the same enslaving mantra until morning broke.

Impromptu

Walter raised his hands from the piano and hummed the last segment of the melody to himself. It was okay, but something was missing. He set it aside in his mind and breathed life into a new chord sequence, thinking,

"Why the fuck am I doing this?"

Outside his bedroom window, a storm was brewing. Nature seemed to laugh at him from a distance. Everything was bleak and gray.

Yet, whenever thoughts like these crossed his mind, it was her mesmerizing voice he heard, echoing the truth a foolish consciousness tried to forget:

"You do it for My amusement, pet."

Yes, always... he would tribute her daily with his musical imagination until his fingers grew numb, or the universe was devoured by silence.

"All for Mistress or nothing at all," he thought as he continued to improvise through the night.

Insidious Virus

Mark's vital signs were dropping fast.

"I don't get it," Diana sobbed. "Why isn't the vaccine working?"

"It's an insidious virus," her mother replied. "It attacks body and mind. You've done all you can for the former. Let's hope the latter remains strong."

"I fucking hate this."

"I know, but all we can do now is wait for him to choose what happens next."

Two days went by without changes. Then, at the morning of the third, Diana found Mark out of bed. He was cleaning the kitchen.

"How long has he been up?" she asked.

"About an hour. In the meantime, he already prepared breakfast and took care of the laundry."

"I guess we now know what he chose."

"True."

"This will take some time getting used to," Diana sighed. The man she used to love was gone forever, only the obedient servant remained.

Inspired

Dr. Elizabeth Harris opened her front door to find her latest patient, June, standing there, smiling.

"What are you doing here?" she asked.

"My apologies, Dr. I know it's not appropriate to show up like this, but I wanted to thank you in person."

"For what?"

"For feeling really inspired after our latest session. That was amazing, thank you!"

"You must be mistaken. I didn't do a thing to you," the hypnotherapist replied.

"My heart knows that's not true although there's something I would like to ask you."

"What is it?"

"I'm not into lesbian anal play and yet wrote a perfect three thousand words scene of a woman being penetrated by her lover's giant black strap-on in twenty minutes. My ass cheeks have been sore all day, too. How do you think that happened?"

"How indeed?" the older woman smirked. "Good night, June. See you next Monday."

"Good night, Dr. Harris. I can't wait."

It's Over

"It's over," Raekelle thought. The hunter's beasts had picked up her scent again, and she couldn't stop the bleeding on her left ankle. She would be captured and sent back to the slave market of Ahnpor if she was lucky. If not, then she would be raped, skinned alive, and eaten before the sun went down.

As the growling sounds drew near, she realized where her erratic running had taken her. The bottom of the valley of Phanys was one of Careth's forbidden places, an unholy magical scar in the world. Only fools ventured there, and few ever returned.

Something unnatural hovered her, flaming red orbs against black skin. Its voice was pure revenge, "Do you want the power to destroy your foes?"

"Yes," Raekelle mumbled, and was immediately consumed by it.

"It's over," she repeated as the first wave of pursuers discovered her location. For them and all men that refused to kneel and worship the darkness within.

Language Barrier

It was past 3 am and Harry couldn't fall asleep, no matter how much he tried. He got up, sat at his laptop, and started browsing random things online. One click led to another, links flared up in quick succession and, before he knew it, he was staring at a strange chat window.

It displayed the following message,

"Tu vais obedecer-me!"

Harry hit the keyboard and typed, "Who are you?"

"Tu vais tornar-te meu escravo!"

"Sorry, but I don't understand what you mean."

Suddenly, his screen started flashing, and rainbow spirals filled the room. He dropped to his knees, never wanting to get up again.

That night, the language barrier wasn't broken, but his mind sure was!

Left to Rot

Philip laid still in bed, listening to Amber's story,

"… and when the prince finally entered the locked room and kissed the princess inside, the spell was broken, and she finally returned to the world of the living. He didn't know at the time she had been trapped there to contain the evil magic within her, but he soon discovered the truth. The moment their eyes met, he was possessed by the need to serve and obey her, no matter the pain she chose to inflict on him."

Philip remained passive as she conjured another needle out of thin air and pierced his balls for the tenth time.

"You really should have left me to rot in that tower," she concluded with an evil grin.

Loading

The loading screen wouldn't budge, and Travis was getting bored.

"Why is it so fucking hard to watch a free video?" he mumbled.

Goddess Victoria's website offered no response. The hypnodomme seemed perfectly content with having an outdated online hub that tested the patience of everyone that stopped by. Random lights flashed at the edges of the screen, and he waited.

One minute went by, then five, and then ten. "Fuck this shit!" he finally said as he prepared to close the browser window.

His fingers froze when her warm voice dripped through his headphones, saying, "Patience will be rewarded. You will be patient, won't you, slave?"

Travis mindlessly agreed, embracing the long wait. The loading of new thoughts inside his brain continued.

Lucky Pet

Madison couldn't stop staring into Barbara's eyes as she weaved her seductive spell around her weakening mind. Perfection was real, and she had found it.

"You love me completely," Barbara said.

"Yes, I do. I love you so fucking much!"

"What will you do for me?"

"What do you want me to do?"

"I really like your car…."

Madison handed her the keys. "It's yours."

"And your apartment…"

"Anything, Goddess."

"And having you sleep in a cage next to my new bed…"

Madison followed her owner to the bedroom and assumed her rightful position. She was such a lucky pet!

Lucky You!

It was a strange question to ask over breakfast, but Paul had no choice. He needed to know.

"Melissa, did you hypnotize me last night?"

"Not last night, nor ever. I told you before I don't do that!"

"Then why can't I stop thinking of strapons?"

"Because deep down you love them? Because they're the thing you've always wanted, the dark desire you simply can no longer live without?"

Paul stared at her, his cock as hard as his mind was soft. Before he could stop himself, he was already dropping to his knees.

"Fuck! Now I need one more than ever!"

"Lucky you! I have one in my purse," she grinned.

Yes, lucky indeed!

May I...?

"Hannah, may I...?"

"No, Frederick."

"Huh? But you didn't even hear what I was about to ask."

"It must be some selfish thing as usual, so no."

"That's not fair."

"Of course, it is. This way, you never get confused because the answer is always 'no'. Now, ask what you were going to ask, anyway."

"Why?"

"Because I gave you an order, and I want to say 'no' again."

"Hannah, may I please be hypnotized by your old pocket watch, today?"

"No..." she smirked before adding. "I have a new one on my leather jacket. Go get it and crawl to me. It better be dangling from your mouth or else..."

Frederick ran to the bedroom, completely ecstatic. God, he loved her so much!

Metamorphosis

Samantha's family was all gathered for the most important night of her life.

"How are you holding up?" her mother asked.

"I'm nervous."

"Understandable, but don't be. It won't take long."

"Will it hurt?"

"Only at the beginning. The pain goes away the moment you stop focusing on it. Ready?"

"I think so."

"Let's get started then."

Samantha kneeled naked in the center of the garden and stretched her palms upward. As the full moon light hit them, her skin began to change, first becoming translucent, then milky white like the cocoon forming around her.

Even in its early stages, she could feel the power of the metamorphosis rewriting reality to please her.

Human? No, she would be a dark angel, a Goddess. All would love and fear her for the rest of their pathetic lives.

Migraines

"Tell me about your migraines," Dr. Rawlins said. "When did they start?"

"At around the same time as my recurring dreams," Jonah replied.

"Oh? And what happens in those dreams?"

"They're always the same. I'm in my room, chained to my bed, and there are half a dozen women dressed in black towering over me. I feel like they're in my head, draining my thoughts one by one. When I wake up, my head hurts like hell, and it won't stop. I need help, Dr."

"Not to worry, I have the right thing for you," she handed him a bottle of purple pills.

"Will they make the migraines or the dreams go away?"

"No, just your memories of what's happening," she thought. Scared meals were the worst.

More than Enough

The succubus stretched in her satin sheet bed. Another morning, another time for a scrumptious meal. Gone were the days of having to blend with the mortal crowd, looking for suitable prey. Technology did all the work for her now. With the press of a button on her smartphone, she recorded a video that immediately set all her social media accounts ablaze.

"Good morning, thralls," she cooed, red tail wrapped around her waist, perfect tits soaking the Winter sun. "It's my birthday, and I'm feeling generous. Today, I'm giving you the chance for you to show Me - Your One and Only Goddess - how much you love and adore Me. The first ten to arrive at my doorstep will have the privilege of being drained. You may lose one or two years of life in the process, but that's a small price to pay compared to the bliss of being at My beck and call, isn't it? Don't keep me waiting."

Less than five minutes later, she had hundreds of men and women salivating by the porch, more than enough to keep her sustained for a couple of months. It's a good thing she had a large basement.

Mysterious Force

No one aboard the Victory knew the contents of the cargo they were transporting, not even the captain, but its effects were felt the moment they left European shores.

As the days and nights went by, one by one, the crew members sank into mindless, ecstatic surrender, dreaming of worshiping an unknown darkness of ancient times with tentacles for hair and shiny black lips. Only one - the cook - resisted the call and chose the icy waters of the Pacific over staying another minute inside the haunted vessel. No one mourned him for how can you cry for something you don't remember?

Two times did a full moon shine upon their obsessed, emaciated faces before it too succumbed to the living darkness. And when the ship came ashore on the New World, the last age of mankind began.

New Appliance

Megan's house never looked cleaner, and her sister Andy was impressed.

"What's your secret?" she asked.

"I got myself a new appliance I'm sure you'll love."

"Can I see it?"

"Sure." Megan snapped her fingers and in came Josh in a surprising attire. "There you go."

"That's just your husband wearing a latex apron."

"Wrong. This is Tex-Bot 2021. It cleans, cooks, gives oral on command, and never complains. It's great."

"That's… surprising. How did you pull that one off?"

"Six months of intense brainwashing. Worth all the hassle though."

"If you say so… Oral on command, huh?"

"Anal too. Want a demonstration?"

"Yes, please."

She got ten, and the day was only starting.

New General

The CyberQueen's drone army was closing in and they were trapped. Jade sat on the cold alleyway and sighed, "I guess this is the end."

"No," Matt replied, reaching for a solitary thermal grenade. "We go down on our terms, not theirs."

"You remembered…"

"Of course, I did. Ready when you are."

"I love you," she held on to his scarred hand.

"I love you, too."

The furious swarm funneled in. Matt flipped them off and activated the explosive.

He died instantly, but Jade's burning body was shot like a cannonball instead, landing a hundred feet away from the detonation site. Bones were shattered and her brain was exposed, yet there was still enough life in her when the first nanites enveloped her.

She will be transformed to serve her true purpose. Long live the CyberQueen's new General!

New Instructions

Gwyn opened her e-mail to read Mistress Brenda's latest message. Her commands were simple,

"Deep sleep now. Repeat your mantra out loud for me. Every time you say it, you'll forget one word until there are none left in your weak mind. Begin."

"I am Mistress Brenda's hypnotized trance slut.

"I am Brenda's hypnotized trance slut.

"am Brenda's hypnotized trance slut.

"am hypnotized trance slut.

"am trance slut.

"am slut.

"slut.

"…"

Gwyn stared vacantly at the screen, waiting for her next instructions. Ten minutes passed, then an hour, half a day…

The weekend is long gone. She's still waiting.

New Vessel

The nanite cloud hovered over Daniel's sunken eyes, a cloud so dense it could be seen with naked eye.

"Don't just stand there, you fool! Run!" Carl screamed from across the street, next to an open manhole.

Daniel looked at him and shrugged, "What's the point? If they don't get us today, they'll get us tomorrow. I'm tired of running. This war has been going on for too long."

"You can't quit!"

"Watch me," he stepped out of the shadows and opened his arms before being swallowed by the metallic storm. In a matter of seconds, his flesh melted, and his now robotized body became yet another vessel for the Drone-Queen's unwavering will.

"Convert," she commanded, deep inside his pulsating brain.

The new unit nodded, and the hunt began.

No Choice

"Remember Hamlet, dear? The most famous passage starts like this: 'to be or not to be…' but the question here is: 'to drain or not to drain your will?'" Angela said as she fiddled with the control panel of her new brainwashing machine.

Sitting behind her, Wanda, her newest acquisition, squirmed against the restraints binding her to the silver chair, but failed to break free.

"I choose drain," Angela smiled wickedly.

The lights flickered in the basement and Wanda never chose anything for herself ever again.

Nothing Changed

The transformation was extreme, and Kyle was flabbergasted.

"Darren? Is that really you?" he asked.

"Of course it's me. How have you been doing?"

"I'm great, but wow! You look so different. How did this happen?"

Darren shrugged. "What are you talking about? Nothing changed since the last time we were together."

"Are you sure?"

"Positive."

"So you've always worn a dress, make-up, wig and heels to the supermarket?"

"I wear them wherever I go, bro. Can't change who I am, right? Anyway, I have to run. Marge is waiting for me outside."

"That explains it," Kyle thought as he remembered his friend's crazy hypnotist ex-girlfriend. She had always wanted a sister, and now she had one.

Little did he know they would become two before the end of the month. He never saw the car that followed him as he headed home.

Performance

I stopped going to the ballet since that strange night, almost four years ago. There I was, sitting at the front row, watching the mesmerizing movements of the dancers when, suddenly, someone whispered in my ear, and I passed out.

When I woke up, the auditorium had been cleared, and I was naked on the center of the stage, slavishly kneeling as twelve ravenous women from ages between eighteen and sixty, had me do all the dancing using nothing my my tongue.

Now, you may think this was just an erotic dream and, for a while, so did I. The video I got in the mail yesterday proves otherwise though and if I don't repeat the performance soon, it will be released to the public. I can't have that.

Time to start practicing again.

Play Ball

Alan entered his mistress' throne room and said,

"Mistress?"

"What is it, slave?"

"I was wondering if… hmm… you would allow me to go play basket with the boys?"

"By boys, you mean your friends?"

"Yes."

"The same friends you were supposed to bring over last time so I could brainwash them, too?"

"Yes."

"Hmm… You may go if you keep your promise this time. If you're not going to, leave and never come back."

"Understood, Mistress. Thank you."

Alan left the room and muttered to himself, "Sorry I have to do this to you guys, but you'll thank me sooner or later."

When the game was over, he drove them all to meet her. It was the last time they played with balls of any shape or size. There's still blood in the room.

Plugged In

Everything was quiet in the Henderson's house when Janine walked in.

"Hailey? I'm here," she said.

Silence. A cold wind blew across the main corridor.

"Hailey? Where are you? We're going to be late for the party."

Janine continued walking around deserted rooms and passageways until she reached a circular space she had never seen before. Hailey sat there waiting for her. The rest of her family stood immobile against the white walls, giant electric plugs sticking out of the base of their pale necks.

"Hey, girlfriend. Do you like it?" Hailey chuckled.

"No! What is this freak show?" Janine asked.

"Oh, they're just rebooting before the celebration. You should too. It's going to be a long night."

A vacant outlet waited for her on the right side of the room. Before she could process what was happening to her, Janine was already plugged in.

"You were always my favorite automaton," Hailey said as her creation's consciousness faded into oblivion once more.

Puzzle Solved

Cameron was confused. Was he winning or what? Point's total said 'yes', but his dwindling thoughts whispered otherwise. He could barely keep his eyes open as Brenda's wheel spun faster and faster inside his mind.

"You're doing great," she purred. "Have you figured out the puzzle yet?"

"Yes," he nodded, eyes glued to the luminous board. Calling the undeniable truth a 'puzzle' was ridiculous, though. The incomplete sentence read,

I _ M _ R E _ _ A' _ H Y _ _ O _ I _ E _ _ O G.

"Say it then."

"I AM BRENDA'S HYPNOTIZED DOG."

"Correct. And you've never been anything else," she concluded.

Cameron nodded and waited for its new collar. Why it had a such human name engraved on it, it would never know.

Reminiscence

Daniel never understood the power of Audrey's black velvet thigh-high socks, but whenever she wore them, his subconscious knew he had to obey her without questioning and go down at her feet, panting like a silly pet in need of attention.

He remembered the shame, the vulnerability, and the relentless ecstasy of going deeper and deeper under her control until his cock and balls became a sticky mess. No matter how many times he told himself it would never happen again, he couldn't stay in control for long.

Those were the days… If only Mistress came back to light up his life again…

Reporting for Duty

"Sergeant Barnes reporting for duty, Ma'am!"

"Welcome back, soldier," Agnes retorted with a fake salute. "I have an assignment of the utmost importance for you. Your former fiancée is in possession of one of my tomes and refuses to return it. You will go to her house right now and retrieve it no matter what. That means no witness if it comes to that, is that clear?"

"Yes, Ma'am! Happy to obey."

"Good. Be on your way then." She laid down the accursed doll on the table and smiled as the reanimated corpse walked out the door.

Retconned

The latest installment of Alicia's favorite horror franchise was the most confusing of all.

"Wasn't she supposed to be his sister?" David asked, munching the last caramel popcorn.

"Only in the second chapter, which was retconned in the fourth," she replied.

"What about the secret society stuff with the horned rings and such?"

"That was only in the fifth movie and the storyline was discarded right after."

"Okay, but I'm pretty sure that character there died in the first act of the third movie."

"In the first rebooted timeline, not the second."

"Fuck! Is there anything in this series that hasn't been rewritten or contradicted at any point?"

"Yes. The assassin always has mind-controlling powers and a boyfriend called David that does the dirty work for her when she's not in the mood. Sounds familiar?"

David's eyes glazed over as he felt the compulsion to head for the kitchen and grab the sharpest knife around. He wouldn't be back home until sunrise.

Reward

"Hop like rabbits!" Mistress Alyssa commanded from her luxurious golden throne. Immediately, half a dozen naked hypnoslaves started jumping around her dungeon, unable to control themselves.

"Good. Now, howl like wolves!"

In unison, they raised their mindless heads high to praise the imaginary moon hanging over them.

"Such good pets…" she chuckled. "Now, fight one another for a chance to lick my pussy."

The howls turned into growls and calm hands into angry claws. There would be blood before pleasure and only one would reap the ultimate reward.

Mistress Alyssa rubbed her hands and waited for the games to finish.

Serve No One

The distorted female voice rang in Janet's ears once again.

"Who do you serve?"

"No one," the blonde teacher replied, her resolve stronger than ever. She would not break.

A surge of electricity ran through the wires connected to her skull, frying yet another part of her brain. She clenched her teeth in pain and stared at the shadow sitting idly behind the brainwashing machine.

"You won't win," she spat.

"You're wrong," the mysterious woman replied, upping the current output. "Who do you serve?"

"No one," Janet coughed as her body convulsed beyond her control.

Gina frowned. Her stepsister was proving to be quite a challenge, but she had all the time in the world to change her ways. Just like everyone else in the family, she would be hers to command, one way or another.

Silver Fantasy

Excerpt from the diary of a fiery redhead mind-controlling magician,

September 27th (night),

"A couple of hours ago, I met a young woman that could pass as my twin outside a bar. The chemistry was off the charts right away and, after a drink or two, she told me her fantasy of becoming a robot.

"To make her wish come true, I got inside her head through her pussy and fired my magic rod. Watching her mind fry before my eyes was a riveting experience, one that never gets old no matter how many times I repeat it.

"Now, all I need is a can of silver paint… This will be great!"

Skipping Ahead

Emily finished scouring Daniel's mind with her magic wand.

"What do you think?" Her younger sister asked.

"Your boyfriend has no thoughts left, Joy. Well done!"

"I told you I was good at this. When can I get my grimoire?"

"You'll need more training before you're given such an honor. Please, be patient."

"For how long? I want to be a full-fledged witch like you!"

"For as long as it takes. The Council will determine when you're ready."

"Isn't there anything I can do to speed the process?"

"No."

"Come on! I know you skipped ahead. How did you do it?"

"Well, I brainwashed my mentor and…"

Emily realized her mistake long before finishing the sentence, but it was already too late.

So Cheap

Ben and Marge couldn't believe their ears when the real estate agent told them the price of the house.

"What? There's no way it's so cheap!" Ben said.

"Unless there's a major catch…" Marge noted. "What is it? Did someone die in here or something?"

"Just a silly urban legend, really," the agent replied. "Some people are convinced there's a ghost around here that possesses women and makes them hypnotize their men into sexual servitude. Isn't that crazy?"

"Definitely," Ben chuckled. "Anyway, cheap or not, I don't like the place, so do you mind showing us another property?"

"Not so fast!" Marge stopped at the base of the stairs and looked up. Something ethereal winked at her, and she grinned. Yes, she definitely wanted that house now…

Status Effect

It was one of the strangest mechanics Alec had ever seen in a video game. In the final dungeon, there was a door with an inscription that read,

"You need to be 25% Entranced to go through."

"That's dumb," he muttered, disabling his character's magical shield. The purple miasma partially dulled his senses, and he pressed on.

In the corridor ahead, laid another door with the same gimmick, except it asked for 50%.

More fog seeped in his brain. The final door had the whooping requirements of 75%, yet he persevered.

Beyond it were the Black Queen's quarters. Alec and his avatar stared in awe at the raven-haired beauty, feelings of endless devotion blooming within.

"You did well making it this far," she said. "Too bad you're now completely powerless to resist me."

As his knees buckled forward, a final message appeared before his eyes showing how easily he had been fooled. It said,

"Don't believe everything you read."

The Nightmare Begins

It had finally happened. After eons of magical imprisonment and almost starving to death more times they could number, the six winged sisters were reunited again. The nightmare was about to begin.

"Everything's so different…" Raelinn mumbled, looking down at the skyscraper jungle where a vast desert plain used to be. "I can't believe those stupid humans were allowed to thrive for so long."

"Worry not, sister, for their reign will soon be over," Vayla retorted. "This world will be ours once more."

"Will you lead us again?" Krinna asked, touching the older alien's left shoulder.

"Always. Let's hunt."

Wings widespread, they descended into the big city, looking for fresh thoughts to consume.

They're Coming

The conclave of monsters and supernatural creatures was gathered for an emergency meeting. The Demon Princess Samhira had awakened once more and had requested an audience.

"How long will you allow humanity to defile our rites?" she asked. "They've turned Halloween into a parody and make fun of our existence with their movies and TV shows! They need to be stopped!"

"What are you proposing?" The leader of the largest pack of werewolves asked.

"Most of them no longer fear us. I'll share with you all my powers of terror and we launch a coordinated attack across the globe to change that."

"What's in it for you?" The oldest vampire queried.

"I want fresh slaves, and scared ones are the best. Do we have a deal?"

"And if we refuse?" the Fairy-Queen frowned.

"You won't leave this room," Samhira declared.

The decision was unanimous. They're coming. Run while you still can.

To Pull a Carrie

Everybody hated Diana, Katya's adopted sister. She was overweight, didn't know when to keep her mouth shut, and was probably a troll or a witch in disguise.

On the day of her eighteenth birthday, a group of Katya's friends got together to pull a Carrie on Diana, a prank that, in their feeble minds, could only be considered cruel if they were in the presence of a real person, which was not the case.

Diana saw the ruse coming from a mile away and discovered her true nature at the same time. Troll? Nah! Witch? Fucking yes!

Everybody loves Diana now, thoughts clouded by her unbreakable spells. They're constantly fighting for her attention, never getting anything in return except contempt. Her birthday is coming up again and there better be good presents. If not, it will be her turn to pull a Carrie and she won't fail.

Ultimate Slave

Angelina couldn't believe what was happening on screen. It was a dream come true.

"Look at this shit!" she pointed at the massive explosions before her eyes. "This game is the best."

"Better than me?" Claire stepped in front of the TV, wearing a skin-tight leather catsuit with generous cleavage.

"Honey, nothing is better than you."

"Good answer," Clara produced a shiny pendant. "You might want to let go of the controller now."

"What do you have in mind?"

"Oh… nothing special, just pushing your buttons so hard you'll even forget your own name while you scream mine and beg for more… are you in?"

Most definitely. She was in and out of trance all weekend, curled like a ball in her powerful yet loving arms. Some girls got to be ultimate warriors, but the lucky ones were ultimate slaves.

Unfair

Zack was on his knees, groveling before his twin sister. He looked pretty pathetic, but she knew he hadn't reached his limit yet.

"Tory, please! I can't take it anymore."

"Sure you can," she smirked, looking down at his disheveled figure. "Locktober only ends next week. You're not getting released sooner no matter what."

"But I didn't consent to this!" he tapped the spiky metal cage that kept his manhood in constant agony.

"Yes, you did," she produced a contract with his handwritten signature at the bottom. "You gave me full control over your cock and balls, bitch!"

"Damn it, Tory! I was hypnotized when you handed me that piece of paper! How's this fair?"

"It's not. Are you done?"

Zack wiped the snot off his nose and gazed into her penetrating blue eyes.

"What do you want me to do?"

"Go get dinner ready. My friends should be here any minute."

He nodded silently and crawled down the stairs, broken beyond repair.

When Nature Fails

Janet slowly destroyed another flower with her sharp nails, thoughts of her boyfriend haunting her mind.

"He loves me; he loves me not; he loves me; he... fuck, he doesn't love me! That won't do."

Up in the sky, the sunlight was slowly fading away. She picked up the shredded petals and descended the mountain back to her cottage and the forbidden book waiting on the table. All the ingredients were accounted for, the only thing missing was his dumb smile right before returning to his rightful state of mind.

Nature had failed her time and time again. Magic never would. Whistling to herself, she began concocting another potion.

You Look Great

"You look great in that costume," Dennis noted, eyes fixed on the green gem dangling between Theresa's breasts.

"And you look adorable with nothing but your collar on..." she smirked, getting ready to straddle his hard cock.

"Thank you, but I'm still not sure how you managed to convince me to wear it though."

The pendant glowed as she moved in for a kiss. "Stop lying to yourself. Your mind knows the truth."

"I don't believe in magic..." he panted, a hint of ripe cherries on her glittering lipstick.

"It still works whether you believe it or not. You never believed in leprechauns either and yet here you are, a slave to one."

"Whatever happened to your pot of gold?" he wet his lips.

"I traded it for the necklace, silly. I told you this story a thousand times already, but you never seem to remember it for long..." she bit his nose, gently.

"Then I don't want to forget again."

"You don't really have a choice in the matter... Happy Halloween, sweetie."

"Happy Halloween, my love."

Conclusion

I hope you enjoyed yourself. This volume may be over, but more are on the way and there are plenty other sexy fantasies waiting for you to explore them of my personal website - https://www.sbspellbound.net. If you haven't visited it yet, this is the perfect opportunity to do so. If you wish for my creative efforts to continue thriving, then please consider supporting them in any way you can. Thanks in advance and see you soon.